Anonymous

The Black Art

Magic Made Easy

Anonymous

The Black Art
Magic Made Easy

ISBN/EAN: 9783337389697

Printed in Europe, USA, Canada, Australia, Japan

Cover: Foto ©Andreas Hilbeck / pixelio.de

More available books at **www.hansebooks.com**

THE BLACK ART
OR
MAGIC
MADE EASY

NEW YORK:

FREDERIC A. BRADY, PUBLISHER,

26 ANN STREET.

THE
LONDON SENSATION

COMIC SONGSTER

Containing popular Songs as sung by J. G. ROBINSON, in the leading
Music Halls in London, Liverpool and New York.

NEW YORK:
FREDERIC A. BRADY, PUBLISHER,
26 ANN STREET.

THE

BLACK ART!

OR,

MAGIC MADE EASY.

Containing a Very Full and Complete Description and

PLAIN EXPLANATION OF

ALL KINDS OF SLEIGHT-OF-HAND TRICKS

AND

CONJURING BY CARDS AND COINS

TOGETHER WITH

WONDERFUL EXPERIMENTS

In Magnetism, Chemistry, Electricity and Fireworks!

So Simplified as to be adapted for Amusement In the Home Circle

NEW-YORK:
FREDERIC A. BRADY, PUBLISHER,
No. 26 ANN STREET.

Contents of The Black Art.

THE BLÂCK ART.

I.—TRICKS WITH CARDS.

1.—How to make the pass.

As what is termed MAKING THE PASS is necessary for performing many of the tricks with cards, the following description of the operation should be well studied.

Hold the pack of cards in your right hand so that the palm of your hand may be under the cards; place the thumb of that hand on one side of the pack; the first, second and third fingers on the other side, and your little finger between those cards that are to be brought to the top and the rest of the pack. Then place your left hand over the cards in such a

manner that the thumb may be at C, the fore-finger
at A, and the other fingers at B, as in the following
figure:—

Bottom.		Top.
2		
Thumb.		
3		
4		
Little Finger.		

The hands and the two parts of the cards being
thus disposed, you draw off the lower cards, confined
by the little finger and the other parts of the right
hand, and place them, with an imperceptible motion,
on the top of the pack,

But before you attempt any of the tricks that de-
pend on MAKING THE PASS, you must have great practice, and be able to perform it so dexterously and ex-
peditiously that the eye cannot detect the movement of
the hand; or you may, instead of deceiving others,
expose yourself.

2.—THE LONG CARD.

Another stratagem, connected with the performance of many of the following tricks, is what is termed the LONG CARD; that is, a card either a trifle longer
or wider than the other cards, not perceptible to the
eye of the spectator, but easily to be distinguished
by the touch of the operator.

3.—To Produce a Particular Card without Seeing the Pack.

Take a pack of cards with the corners cut off. Place them all one way, and ask a person to draw a card; when he has done so, while he is looking at it, reverse the pack, so that when he returns the card to the pack, the corner of it will project from the rest; let him shuffle them ; he will never observe the projecting card. Hold them behind your back. You can feel the projecting card—draw it out, and show it. Simple as this trick is, it will excite great astonishment.

4.—To Call for Any Card in the Pack.

This is a very simple trick, but will greatly astonish an audience to whom it is not known. Seat yourself at a table, so as to have the whole of the company as much as possible in front of you and at some distance. Take the pack of cards as it usually lies, and, in passing it under the table or behind you, glance at the card which happens to be exposed; then, pretending to shuffle the cards, place the one you have seen, back to back on the other side of the pack, and holding the cards firmly by the edges, raise your hand between you and the company, and show the card you have seen, calling out, at the same time, what it is.

Observe which card is facing you (for you have now the whole pack facing you, except the one card which is shown to the spectators), pass them under the table again, and transfer the card you have just seen to the other side of the pack, handling the cards as if shuffling them ; again exhibit, and cry out the

name of the card turned to the company, taking care
to notice the card that faces yourself, which change
as before, and so on.   By this means you may go
over the whole pack, telling each card as it is exposed,
without looking at the cards, except when they are
held up between you and the spectators, and when
they are anxiously looking at them themselves, to see
whether you are right or not.

5.—THE CHANGEABLE ACE.

Take the Ace of Diamonds, and place over it with
paste or soap, so as to slip off easily, a club cut out
of thin paper, so as to entirely conceal it. After
showing a person the card, you let him hold one end
of it, and you hold the other, and while you amuse
him with discourse, you slide off the heart.   Then
laying the card on the table, you bid him cover it wi h
his hand; you then knock under the table, and command the club to turn into the Ace of Diamonds.

6.—THE CONVERTIBLE ACES.

This trick is similar to the foregoing.   On the Ace
of Spades fix a heart, and on the Ace of Hearts a
S a le, in the manner already described.

Show these two Aces to the company; then, taking
the Ace of Spades, you desire a person to put his foot
upon it, and as you place it on the ground draw
away the S a le.   In like manner you place the seeming Ace of Hearts under the foot of another person.
You then command the two cards to change their
places; and that they obey your command, the two
persons, on taking up their cards, will have occular
demonstration.

7.—THE GATHERING OF THE CLANS.

Have in readiness a pack of cards, all the cards of which are arranged in successive order; that is to say, if it consists of fifty-two cards, every thirteen must be regularly arranged, without a duplicate of any one of them. After they have been cut (do not suffer them to be shuffled) as many times as a person may choose, form them into thirteen heaps of four cards each, with the colourd faces downwards, and put them carefully together again. When this is done, the king, the four knaves, the four queens, and so on, must necessarily be together.

8.—EVERYBODY'S CARD.

Provide a pack in which there's a long card; open it at that part where the long card is and present the pack to a person in such a manner that he will naturally draw that card. After telling him to put it into any part of the pack, you shuffle the cards. Then take the pack and offer the same card to a second or third person, taking care that they do not stand near enough to see the card each other draws.

Draw several cards yourself, among which is the long card, spread them, or show them, and ask each of the parties if this card be among these cards, and he will naturally auswer yes, as they have all drawn the same card. You then shuffle all the cards together, and cutting them at the long card, you hold it before the first person, so that the others may not see it, and tell him that is his card. Return it to the pack, shuffle and cut them again at the same card, and hold it to the second person, and so of the rest.

9.—FORCING A CARD.

By forcing a card you compel a person to take such a card as you think fit, while he imagines he is taking one hap-hazard, or according to his own choice. It is almost impossible to describe accurately the method of performing this trick, but it is as follows:—Ascertain secretly, or whilst you are amusing yourself with the cards, what the one is which you intend to force, place it in the pack, but keep your eye, on the little finger of your left hand, in which you hold the pack, upon it. Next desire a person to select a card from the pack, for which purpose you must open it quickly from left to right, spreading the cards backwards and forwards so as to perplex his choice, and when you see him about to take one, open the pack until you come to that one which you intend him to have, and, just at the moment his fingers are touching the pack, let its corner project invitingly a little forwards in front of the others; this will seem so fair that in nine cases out of ten he will take the one so offered, unless he is himself quite aware of the secret of forcing. Having by this method forced your card, you may request him to examine it, and then give him the pack to shuffle, which he may do as often as he likes, for you are of course always aware what card he has taken. A perfect knowledge of forcing is indispensably necessary before you attempt the more difficult tricks with cards.

10.—THE CARD HIT UPON BY GUESS.

Spread part of a pack before a person, in such a way that only one court card is visible, and arrange that it shall appear the most prominent and striking card. You desire him to think on one, and observe if he fixes his eye on the court card. When he tells you he has determined on one, shuffle the cards, and turn them up one by one, when you come to the court card, tell him that is the one. If he does not seem to fix his eye on the court card, you should not hazard the experiment, but frame an excuse for performing some other amusement, this trick should not be attempted with those who are conversant with this sort of deception.

11.—Ups and Downs.

This is a very simple way of ascertaining what card a person chooses. When you are playing with the pack, drop out the diamonds, from the ace to the ten, and contrive, without being perceived, to get all the other cards with their heads in the same direction; then request a person to choose a card: do not FORCE one, but let him choose whichever he pleases: while he has it in his hand and is looking at it, carelessly turn the pack in your hand, so that the position of the cards may be reversed; then bid him put the card he has chosen into the centre of the pack: shuffle and cut them, and you may to a certainty know the card chosen, by its head being upside down, or in a different direction from the rest of the pack.

12.—To tell the Card that a Person has touched with his Finger.

This amusement has to be performed by confederacy. You previously agree with your confederate on certain signs, by which he is to denote the suite, and

the particular card of each suite ; thus :—if he touch
the first button of his coat, it signifies an ace; if the
second a king, &c. ; and then again, if he take out
this handkerchief, it denotes the suite to be hearts; if
he takes snuff, diamonds, &c. These prel'm'naries
being settled, you give the pack to a person who is
near your confederate, and tell him to separate any
one card from the rest while you are absent, and
draw his finger once over it. He is then to return
you the pack, and while you are shuffling the cards,
you carefully note the signals made by your confederate; then turning the cards over one by one, you
directly fix on the card he touched.

13.—THE CARD DISCOVERED BY TOUCH OR SMELL.

Offer the long card, or any other that you thoroughly well know, and as the person who has drawn it
holds it in his hand, pretend to feel the pips or
figures on the under side with your forefinger, or
smell it, and then sagaciously declare what card it is.

If it is the long card you may give the pack to the
person who drew it, and allow him either to replace it
or not. The take the pack, and feel whether it is
there or not; shuffle the cards in a careless manner,
and, without looking at it, decide accordingly.

14.—CONFEDERATE CARDS.

Request a person to draw four cards from the pack,
and tell him to remember one of them. He then returns them to the pack, and you dexterously place
two under and two on the top of the pack. Under
the bottom ones you place four cards of any sort, and
then, taking eight or ten from the bottom cards you

spread them on the table, and ask the person if the card he fixed on be among them. If he say no, you may be sure that it is one of the two cards on the top. You then pass those two cards to the bottom, and drawing off the lowest of them, you ask if that is not his card. Should he again say no, you take up that card, and bid him draw his card from the bottom of the pack. But if, on the contrary, he says his cards are among those you first drew from the bottom, you must dexterously take up the four cards you put under them, and placing those on the top, let the other two be the bottom cards of the pack, which you are to draw in the manner before described.

15.—THE TEN DUPLICATES, OR CARDS IN COUPLES.

Select any twenty cards. Let any person shuffle them; lay them in pairs upon the table without looking at them. You next desire several persons (as many persons as there are pairs on the table) to look at different pairs, and remember what cards compose them. You then take up all the cards in the order in which they have been laid, and replace them with their faces uppermost upon the table, according to the situation of the letters in the following word:—

M	U	T	U	S
1	2	3	4	5
D	E	D	I	T
6	7	8	9	10
N	O	M	E	N
11	12	13	14	15
C	O	C	I	S
16	17	18	19	20

These words, which have no particular meaning, contain ten letters repeated, or two of each sort. You therefore ask each person which row or rows the cards he looked at are in; if he says the first, they must be the second and forth in that row, these being the only duplicates or two letters of the same (U's) in them; if he says the second and fourth, they must be the ninth and nineteenth (two I's), and so of all the rest. This amusement, which is very simple, and requires very little practice, will excite considerable astonishment in those unacquainted with the key.

16.—THE TURN-OVER FEAT.

Having found a card chosen which you have previously forced, or any card that has been drawn, which you have discovered by the means before described, in order to do the feat cleverly, convey the card privately to the top of the pack; get the rest of the cards even with each other, making the edge of the top card project a little over the others; then, holding them between your finger and thumb, about two feet from the table, let them drop, and the top card which as has been said, must be the one drawn will fall face uppermost, and all the others with their faces towards the table.

17.—THE NERVE FEAT.

Force a card, and request the person who has taken it to put it in the pack, and shuffle the cards; then look at them again yourself, find the card, and place it at the bottom; cut them in two parts: give him the part containing his card at the bottom, and desire him to hold it between his finger and thumb just at the corner; after telling him to hold them tight, strike them sharply, and they will all fall to the ground, except the bottom one, which is the card he has chosen. It is an improvement in this feat to put the chosen card at the top of the pack, and turn the cards face upwards so that when you strike, the chosen party's card will remain in his hand, staring him in the face.

18.—To tell the Number of Cards by the Weight.

Take a parcel of cards, say forty, and privately insert amongst them two long cards; let the first be for example, the fifteenth, and the other the twenty-sixth, from the top. Seem to shuffle the cards, and cut them at the first long card; poise those you have taken off in your hand, and say, "There must be fifteen cards here;" then cut them at the second long card, and say, "There are but eleven here;" and poising the remainder, exclaim, "And here are fourteen cards." On counting them, the spectators will find your calculations correct.

19.—To Change the Card by Word of Command.

You must have two cards of the same sort in the pack, the King of Spades. Place one next the bottom card, (say, the Seven of Hearts,) and the other at the top. Shuffle the cards without displacing those three, and show a person that the bottom card is the Seven of Hearts. This card you dexterously slip aside

with your finger, which you have previously wetted.
and taking the King of Spades from the bottom,
which the person supposes to be the Seven of Hearts,
lay it on the table, telling him to cover it with his
hand. Shuffle the cards again, without displacing
the first and last card, and shifting the other King of
Spades from the top to the bottom, show it to another person. You then draw that privately away,
and taking the bottom card, which will then be the
Seven of Hearts, you lay that on the table, and tell
the second person (who believes it to be the King of
Spades,) to cover it with his hand. You then command the cards to change places, and when the two
parties take off their hands and turn up the cards,
they will see, to their great astonishment, that your
commands are obeyed.

21.—THE CARD IN A MIRROR.

Get a round mirror; frame size of a card. Make the glass in
the middle move in the two groves A B and C D and the

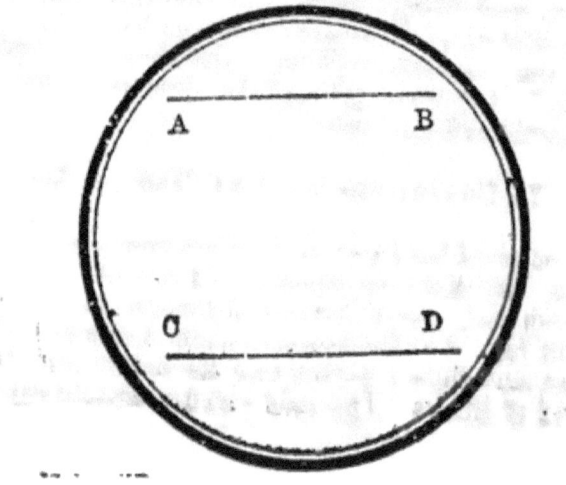

quicksilver must be scraped off equal to the size of a card. The glass must also be wider than the distance between the frame by the width of a card. Then cement a piece of pasteboard, on which is a card that must exactly fit the space, over the part where the quicksilver is rubbed off. This card must at first be placed behind the frame.

Secure the mirror against a partition, through which are to go two strings, by pulling which an assistant can easily move the glass in the grooves, and consequently make the card appear or disappear at pleasure.

The assistance of a confederate is not absolutely necessary to this performance. A table may be placed under the mirror, and the string be made to pass through a leg, communicating with a small trigger, to be pushed down by the foot; taking occasion to dust the glass with your handkerchief, as if it were intended to make the card appear the more conspicuous.

22. THE CARD IN THE OPERA-GLASS.

Procure an opera-glass two inches and a half long; the tube to be made of ivory so thin that it may not appear opaque. Place it in a magnifying glass of such a power, and at such a distance, that a card three-quarters of an inch long may appear like a common-sized card.

At the bottom of the tube lay a circle of black pasteboard, to which fasten a small card, with the pips or figures on both sides, and in such a manner that, by turning the tube, either side of the glass may be visible.

You then offer two cards to two persons similar to the double card in the glass. You put them in the pack again, or convey them into your pocket; and after a few flourishing motions, you tell the persons you have conveyed their cards into the glass; then you show each person his card in the glass by turning it in the proper position.

You may easily induce the parties to draw the two cards you wish by placing them first on the top of the pack, and then, by making the pass, bringing them to the middle. When you can make the pass in a dexterous manner, it is preferable to the long card, which obliges the operator to change the pack frequently, as, if the same card is always drawn, it may excite suspicion.

23.—THE CARDS IN TEA-CADDIES.

Two cards being drawn by different persons, are put into separate tea-caddies and locked up. The performer changes the cards without touching them, or any confederacy. The caddies are made with a copper flap, which has a hinge at the bottom, opens against the front, where it catches under the bolt of the lock, so that, when the lid is shut and locked, the flap will fall down upon the bottom; the performer places two cards that he intends to be chosen between the flap and the front, which, being lined with green cloth, may be handled without any suspicion; he then desires the first person to put his card into one of the caddies, taking care it be that which contains the contrary card to the one that he chose, and the second into the other; he then desires they will lock them up, which unlocks the flaps, covers their cards, and, when opened, presents the contrary ones to the view of the company.

24.—TO CHANGE A CARD THAT'S BEEN PUT IN A BOX.

A box must be made on purpose, with a double bottom, and upon the false one is to be laid the card which the first person chooses. In locking the box, by a secret spring the false bottom is raised with the card, and firmly united with that part where the hinges are. On the real bottom lies another card, which had been previously and secretly deposited there.

In making a person draw a card, a duplicate of this is forced upon him; for if he attempts to draw another, under some pretence you shuffle the cards again, till at last he takes the very card you intended for him. This card you know by feeling it, it being purposely longer than any of the rest, and is in fact a conjurer's secret card. You must never let one of these particular or trick cards remain in a pack when you give it to be examined.

25.—To pick out a Card thought of, Blindfold.

Take twenty-one cards, and lay them down in three rows, with their faces upwards; I. E. when you have laid out three, begin again at the left hand, and lay one card upon the first, and so on to the right hand ; then begin on the left hand again, and so go on until you have laid out the twenty-one cards in three heaps, at the same time requesting any one to think of a card. When you have laid them out, ask him which heap his card is in; then lay that heap in the middle between the other two. This done, lay them out again in three heaps as before, and again request him to notice where his noted card goes, and put that heap in the middle, as before. Then taking up the cards with their backs toward you, take off the uppermost card, and reckon it one; take off another, which reckon two; and thus proceed till you come to the eleventh, which will invariably prove to be the card thought of. You must never lay out your cards less than three times, but as often above that number as you please. This trick may be done without your seeing the cards at all, if you handle and count them carefully. To diversify the trick, you may use a different number of cards, but the number chosen must be divisible by three, and the middle card, after they have been thrice dealt as directed, will always be the one thought of; for instance, if done with fifteen cards, it must be the eighth, and so on ; when the number is even, it must be the exact half; as, if it be twenty-four, the card thought of will be the twelfth, &c.

26.—THE KNAVES AND THE CONSTABLE.

Pick the four knaves out of a pack of cards, and one of the kings to perform the office of constable. Secretly place one of the knaves at the bottom of the pack, and lay the other three with the constable down upon the table. Amuse the spectators with a tale of three knaves one going to rob a house; one got in at the parlor window (putting a knave at the bottom of the pack, taking care not to lift the pack so high that the one already at the bottom can be seen), one effected his entrance at the first-floor window (putting another knave in the middle of the pack), and the other by getting on the parapet from a neighbouring house, contrived to scramble in at the garret-window (placing the third knave at the top of the pack); the constable vowed he would capture them, and closely followed the last knave (putting the king likewise upon the top of the pack). You then request as many of the company to cut the cards as please, and tell them that you have no doubt the constable has succeeded in his object, which will be apparent when you spread out the pack in your hands, as the king and three knaves will, if the trick is neatly performed, be found together. A very little practice only is required to enable you to convey a knave or any other card secretly to the bottom of the pack.

27.—THE ROYAL EMIGRANTS.

Take the twelve court cards (knaves, kings, queens),

from the pack, and place them in three rows, four in each. Commencing with the fourth card in the bottom row on the right, take them up LONGWAYS, ONE OVER THE OTHER, and offer them to any of the company to cut. It is of no consequence how often they are divided. Next deal them out in four divisions, and the king, queen, and knave of each suit will be found together.

The key to this mystery consists in observing the following arrangements in the disposition of the cards at first:

Place one of each suit in the upper row, begin the next row with a card of the same suit that you left off with in the first, and commence the third or last row with a court card of the same suit that you left off with in the second.

On following the above directions in taking up the cards, the result will be as described.

28.—TO SHUFFLE CARDS SO AS ALWAYS TO KEEP ONE CERTAIN CARD AT THE BOTTOM.

In showing tricks with cards, the principal point consists in shuffling them nimbly, and keeping one certain card either at the bottom, or in some known place of the pack four or five cards from the bottom; for by this you may seem to work wonders, since it is easy for you to see or take notice of a card, which, though you are perceived to do, it will not be suspected, if you shuffle them well together afterwards, by the method here taught, which is this: in shuffling, let the bottom card be always kept a little before, or, which is best, a little behind all the rest of the cards; put it a little beyond the rest before, right over your forefinger, or else, which is best, a little behind the rest, so that the little finger of the left hand may slip up and meet with it at the first shuffle; then throw upon the board the bottom card, with as many more as you would preserve for any purpose, a little before or a little behind the rest; and be sure to let your forefinger, if the pack be laid before, or your little finger, if the pack be laid behind, always creep up to meet with the bottom card; when you feel it, you may there hold it till you have shuffled over again, which being done, the card which was first at the bottom will come there again; then you may shuffle them before the spectators, and yet leave your noted card at the bottom. You must try to be perfect in this method of shuffling, as, having once attained it, you may do almost what you please; for whatever pack you make, though it is ten, or twelve, or twenty cards, you may still keep it next the bottom, and yet shuffle them often to please the curious.

29.—The Magic Opera-Glass.

Before you begin to perform this extraordinary illusion, prepare a table of figures exactly like the following:

1,181	10,132	19,133
2,231	11,232	20,233
3,331	12,332	21,333
4,121	13,122	22,123
5,221	14,222	23,223
6,321	15,322	24,323
7,111	16,112	25,113
8,211	17,212	26,213
9,311	18,312	27,313

This magical arithmetical combination you may fix in an opera-glass, or the crown of your hat, as occasion may serve. Take a pack of cards, consisting of twenty-seven only, and give them to a person; desire him to fix on any one, then shuffle them, and return the pack to you.

Place the twenty-seven cards in three heaps, by laying down one alternately on each heap; but before you put each card down, show it to the person, without seeing it yourself. When the three equal heaps are completed, ask him at what number from twenty-seven he will have his card appear, and in which heap it is. Now look at your magic table, and if the first of three numbers which stand against that number it is to appear at, be one, put that heap AT TOP; if the number be two, put it in the middle, and if three, put it at the bottom. Then divide the card into three heaps in the same manner a second and a third time, and his card will be at the number he chose. For the sake of making the elucidation perfectly clear, we will give an example: Suppose he desire that his card shall be the twentieth from the top, and the first time of making the heaps he says it is in the third heap. You then look through your opera-glass at the magic table and see that the first figure against the number twenty is two. You therefore put that heap in the middle of the pack. The second and third times you in like manner put the heap in which he says it is at the bottom, the succeeding numbers both being three. Now, laying the cards down one by one, the twentieth card will be that he fixed on. You may, of course, in like manner, show the person his card without asking him at what number it shall appear, by fixing on any number yourself. By the same table a variety of tricks equally surprising can be performed, only requiring the exercise of a little ingenuity.

80.—To Separate the Two Colors of a Pack of Cards by One Cut.

To perform this trick, all the cards of one color must be cut a little narrower at one end than the other. You show the cards, and give them to any one that he may shuffle them; then, holding them between your hands, one hand being at each extremity, with one motion you separate the hearts and diamonds from the spades and clubs.

81.--The Card Discovered Under the Handker-chief.

Let a person draw any card from the rest, and put it in the middle of the pack; you make the pass at that place, and the card will consequently be at the top; then placing the pack on the table, cover it with a handkerchief, and putting your hand under it, take off the top card, and after seeming to search among the cards for some time, draw it out.

This amusement may be performed by putting the cards in another person's pocket, after the pass is made.

Several cards may also be drawn and placed together in the middle of the pack, and the pass then made.

82.—THE CARD UNDER THE HAT.

This wonderful trick is performed in the same manner as is directed for finding a card placed under a
handkerchief.

33.—THE CARD BURNED AND AFTERWARDS FOUND IN A WATCH.

Ask one of the company to draw a chance card,
and then procure three watches from the spectators,
which you wrap up in separate pieces of paper in the
form of dice-boxes, which are laid upon a table and
covered with a napkin; the card chosen is burned,
and the cinders put in a box; shortly after the box is
opened, and the ashes are not there. The three
watches are put on a plate, and you ask one of the
company to choose one; the same person opens the
watch, and finds under the glass a piece of the burned
card, and in the watch-case, under the watch, will
be found a miniature card resembling the one burnt.
To accomplish this trick, you must carefully observe
the following directions:—When you have made
known to the confederate the card chosen, he stretches
his arm into the table to take one of the watches, and
deposit there what is requisite; the watches must be
covered with a napkin, which is supported by bottles,
or something else, otherwise the hand of the confederate would be seen, or the napkin would be perceived
to move. As for the means employed to cause the
ashes of the burnt card to disappear in the box, it consists in putting into the cover a piece of wood or paper
which exactly fits it, and falls down to the bottom

when the box is shut; this piece of wood or paper being of the same color as the inside of the box, operates as a double bottom, and hides the ashes from the view of the deceived spectator, who at that moment is tempted to believe that the ashes are gone out to be combined anew, and to produce the miniature card which is to be found in the watch.

34.--THE CARD IN THE NUT.

Bore a hole in a nut with a small gimlet, and with a pin break and extract the kernel Draw the spots of a card on a piece of thin paper, then roll this miniature card into as small a compass as possible, and put it into the nut. Stop the hole up with wax, which rub over with a little dust, so that it may not be noticed. Let some one draw a card, and take care that it be the same as that marked on the paper ; when he has returned the card to the pack, desire him to crack the nut, in which he will find his card.

35.—THE CARD IN THE EGG.

Take a card, the same as your long card, and rolling it up very close, put it in an egg, by making a hole as small as possible, and which you are to fill up carefully with white wax. You then offer the long card to be drawn, and when it is replaced in the pack you shuffle the cards several times, giving the egg to the person who drew the card ; and while he is breaking it, you privately withdraw the long card, that it may appear on examining the cards to have gone from the pack into the egg. This may be rendered more surprising by having several eggs, in each of which is placed a card of the same sort, and then giving the person the liberty to choose which egg he thinks fit.

This diversion may be still further diversified by having, as most public performers have, a confederate, who is previously to know the egg in which the card is placed ; for you may then break the other eggs, and show that the only one that contains a card is that in which you directed it to be.

86—The Card in the Pocket-Book.

A confederate is previously to know the card you have taken from the pack and put into your pocket-book. You then present the pack to him, and force one in the usual way (which we will suppose to be the King of Hearts), and place the pack on the table. You then ask him the name of the card, and when he says the King of Hearts, you ask him if he is not mistaken, and if he be sure that the card is in the pack ; when he replies in the affirmative, you say, " It might be there when you looked over the cards, but I believe it is now in my pocket ;" then desire a third person to put his hand in your pocket, and take out your book, —when it is opened the card will appear.

37.—The Card Found Out by the Point of a Sword.

When a card has been drawn, you place it under the long card, and by shuffling them dexterously you bring it to the top of the pack. Then lay or throw the pack on the ground, observing where the top card lies. A handkerchief is then bound round your eyes, which ought to be done by a confederate, in such a way that you can see the ground. A sword is then put in your hand, with which you touch several of the cards, as if in doubt, but never losing sight of the top card, in which at last you fix the point of the sword, and present to the party who drew it.

38.—To Select all the Court Cards Blindfold.

The following trick is one of the simplest when known, but excites great wonder in a private party during its operation.

Previous to your wishing to perform this trick, draw aside one of the party, and make him acquainted with the process of it. After mingling again with the company, and introducing a discourse about various tricks with cards, you may then profess to have the power of picking out all the court cards blindfold.

The process is this: After your eyes are tightly bound, and the company seem perfectly satisfied that they are so, take up the pack, and, holding up one in view of the whole company, feel it about. Your confederate, whom you contrive to have seated next to you, if a court card, must then tread on your toes, and you proclaim aloud, "Ah! this is a good one!" You then hold up another card, feeling and smelling it all over, and if it prove a common card, your confederate takes no notice of it; you then say, "No, this will not do; this is a bad one;" and so on, till you have convinced the company of your capability.

39.—To Name the Card upon which One or more Persons Fix.

There must be as many different cards shown to each person as there are cards to choose; so that, if

there are three persons, you must show three cards to
each person, telling the first to retain one in his mem-
ory. You then lay the three cards down, and show
three others to the second person, and three others to
the third.   Next, take up the first person's cards, and
lay them down separately one by one, with their faces
upwards; place the second person's cards over the
first, and the third over the second's, so that there
will be one card in each parcel belonging to each person.

Then ask each of them in which parcel his card is,
for the first person's will always be first, the second
person's the second, and the third person's the third,
in that parcel where each says his card is.   This
amusement may be performed with a single person,
by letting him fix on three, four, or more cards.   In
this case you must show him as many parcels as he is
to choose cards, and every parcel must consist of that
number out of which he is to fix on one, and you then
proceed as before, he telling you the parcel that contains each of his cards.

40.—To Make the Court Cards always Come Together.

Take the pack, and separate all the kings, queens
and knaves.   Put these all together into any part of
the pack you fancy, and inform one of the company
that he cannot in twelve cuts disturb their order.   The
chances are 500 to 1 in your favor; but with a novice
the feat becomes impossible.   This is a very amusing
and easy trick.

This trick may also be rendered more wonderful by

placing one half of the above number of cards at the bottom and the other at the top of the pack.

41.—To Change Four Knaves or Kings Held in Your Hand into Blank Cards or into Four Aces.

You must have cards made for the purpose of this feat—half cards, as they may be properly termed—that is, one half kings or knaves, and the other half aces. When you lay the aces one over the other, nothing but the kings or knaves will be seen. Then turning the kings or knaves downwards, the four aces will be seen. You must have two perfect cards, one a king or knave, to cover one of the aces, or else it will be seen; and the other an ace to lay over the kings or knaves. When you wish to make them all blank cards, lay the cards a little lower, and, by hiding the aces, they will all appear white on both sides. You may then ask the company which they choose; exhibit kings, aces, or blanks as required.

42—Picture Cards.

Take a dozen or more plain cards. and draw a line from the right-hand upper corner to the left-hand lower corner of the face of each, so that the cards will be equally divided by the lines; then, on the right-hand half, paint any description of subjects, such as flowers, birds, grotesque figures, heads, &c., leaving the left-hand half blank. By adroit shuffling, showing only half of the cards at one time, you may, to all appearance, transform plain cards into painted ones, or painted into plain.

84.—THE LOCOMOTIVE CARD.

This will appear a marvelous trick if well performed. Take a pack of cards, and let any person draw one from it, tell him to look on the card, that he may know it again, and then put it into the pack. Hold the pack so that the person may place his card in it, making sure that you hold the card next to the bottom open for him to place his card in, manœuvring the cards well, that he may imagine he has placed his card in the mlddle of the pack: by this means you know where the card is, and when you are shuffling them, you can very easily place the particular card on the top of the pack. Then take a piece of wax with a long hair attached to it, fastening it to the bottom of your vest (it must be prepared before you commence the trick), have the wax placed under the thumb-nail of your right hand, and stick it to the card that was drawn; spread the cards on the table, then asking the person to name the card he selected, command it to move from the pack to your hand. By shifting your position backwards, the card will move also.

44.—THE PAINTED PACK.

On the backs of half a pack of cards paint a variety of different subjects, and on the faces of the other half of the pack paint similar subjects, so that between them you will have a complete pack of pictorial designs. Show the faces of those cards which have their backs painted, and, by cleverly shuffling, you may make it appear as if you transformed them into a series of grotesque figures, and so create much laughter. In performing this trick the cards must be shown only half way. Another method of making a painted pack is to take a dozen or more plain cards, and draw a line from the right-hand upper corner to the left-hand lower corner of the face of each of them—by which line they will be equally divided —and delineate in the right-hand division of each card some comical figure, leaving the left-hand division blank. By clever management in shuffling you may, to all appearance, transform what seem plain cards into a painted pack.

45.—To Turn a Card into a Bird.

Having a live bird in your sleeve, take a card in your hand, exhibit it, and then draw it into your sleeve with your thumb and little finger, giving the arm a shake sufficient to bring the bird into your hand, which you may then produce and let fly.

46.—Cards Changing Places by Command.

You must have two cards of the same sort in the same pack, say the Queen of Clubs. Place one next the bottom card, say the Ten of Diamonds, and the other at top. Shuffle the cards without displacing these three, and show a person that the bottom card is the Ten of Diamonds. This card you dextrously slip aside with your finger, which you have previously wetted, and taking the Queen of Clubs from the bottom, which the person supposes to be the Ten of Diamonds, lay it on the table, telling him to cover it with his hand. Shuffle the cards again, without displacing the first and last card, and shifting the other Queen of Clubs from the top to the bottom, show it to another person. You then draw that privately away, and taking the bottom card, which will then be the Ten of Diamonds, you lay that on the table, and tell the second person, who believes it to be the Queen of Clubs, to cover it with his hand. You then command the cards to change places : and when the two parties take off their hands, and turn up the cards, they will see, to their great astonishment, that your commands are obeyed.

47.—To Produce a Mouse from a Pack of Cards.

Have a pack of cards fastened together at the edges, but open in the middle like a box, a whole card being glued on as the cover, and many loose ones placed above it, which require to be dexterously shuffled, so that the entire may seem a real pack of cards. The bottom must likewise be a whole card, glued to the box on one side only, yielding immediately to interior pressure, and serving as a door by which you convey the mouse into the box. Being thus prepared, and holding the bottom tight with your hand, request one of the company to place his open hands together, and tell him you mean to produce something very marvellous from the pack of cards; place the pack in his hands, and while you engage his attention in conversation, affect to want something out of your bag, and at the same moment take the pack by the middle, and throw it into the bag; then the mouse will remain in the hands of the person who held the cards.

48.—To Name the Rank of a Card that a Person has Drawn from a Piquet Pack.

The rank of a card means whether it be an ace, king, queen, &c. You therefore first fix a certain number to each card; thus, you call the king four, the queen three, the knave two, the ace one, and the others according to the number of their pips.

Shuffle the cards, and let a person draw any one of them; then turning up the remaining cards, you add the number of the first to that of the second, the second to the third, and so on, till it amounts to ten, which you then reject, and begin again; or if it be more, reject the ten, and carry the remainder to the next card, and so on to the last; to the last amount add four, and subtract that sum from ten if it be less, or from twenty if it be more than ten, and the remainder will be the number of the card that was drawn; as for example, if the remainder be two, the card drawn was a knave; if three, a queen, and so on.

49.—To Tell the Card that May be Noted.

Take several cards, say ten or twelve; remember how many there are, and hold them up with their backs towards you; open four or five of the uppermost, and while you hold them out, request some person to note a card, and tell you whether it is the first, second, or third from the top; when he has informed you, shut up the cards in your hand, place the remainder of the pack upon them, and tap their ends and sides upon the table, so as to make it seem impossible to find the card in question. It may, how-

ever, be easily found thus: subtract the number of
cards you had in your hand from fifty-two, which is
the number of the pack, and to the remainder add
the number of the noted card, and you will instantly
have the number of the noted card from the top.

50.—To Tell the Amount of the Numbers of any Two Cards Drawn from a Common Pack.

Each court card in this case counts for ten, and the
other cards according to the number of their pips.
Let the person who draws the cards add as many
more cards to each of of those he has drawn as will
make each of their numbers twenty-five. Then take
the remaining cards in your hand, and, seeming to
search for some card among them, tell them over to
yourself, and their number will be the amount of the
two cards drawn.

For example—Suppose a person has drawn a ten
and a seven; then he must add fifteen cards to the
first, to make the number twenty-five, and eighteen
to the last, for the same reason. Now, fifteen and
eighteen make thirty-three, and the two cards themselves make thirty-five, which, deducted from fifty-two,
leaves seventeen, which must be the number of the remaining cards, and also of the two cards drawn.

You may perform this amusement without touching the cards, thus:

Let the person who has drawn the two cards deduct
the number of each of them from twenty-six, which is
half the number of the pack; and, after adding the
remainders together, let him tell you the amount,

which you privately deduct from fifty-two, the total number of all the cards, and the remainder will be the amount of the two cards.

EXAMPLE.—Suppose the two cards to be as before, ten and seven ; then the person deducting ten from twenty-six, there remains sixteen, and taking seven from twenty-six, there remains nineteen ; these two remainders added together make thirty-five, which you substract from fifty-two, and there must remain seventeen for the amount of the two cards, as before.

51.—TEN CARDS BEING ARRANGED IN A CIRCLE, TO TELL THAT WHICH ANY ONE THOUGHT OF.

Arrange the spotted cards of any suit, that is from one to ten, in a circular form, as in the annexed diagram. Ask a person to think of a number or card, and to touch also any other number or card ; desire him to add to the number of the card he touched the number of the cards laid out—that is, ten— and then bid him count that sum backwards, beginning at the card he touched, and reckoning that card at the number he thought of: by counting thus he will end it at the card or number he first thought of, and thereby enable you to ascertain what that was. For example, suppose he thought of the number three, and touched the sixth card, if ten be added to six, it will of course

make sixteen; and if he counts that number from
the sixth card, the one touched, in a retrograde order, reckoning three on the sixth, four on the fifth,
five on the fourth, six on the third cards, and so on,
it will be found to terminate on the third card, which
will therefore show you the number the person
thought of. When the person is counting the numbers he should not, of course, call them out aloud.

52.—A New Method to Tell a Card by its Weight.

You declare to the company that you can tell a
card by weighing it. You take the pack in your
hand, let one of the company draw a card, look at it,
and place it face downwards in your hand. You
then look at it attentively, apparently trying its
weight, while in fact you are examining it very
closely, to see if you cannot discern upon its back
some mark by which you may know it again, and if
there is none you mark it secretly with your nail.

You let the person put the card in the pack, shuffle
it, and hand it back to you. You now look through
the pack, take one card after another, and appear as
if you were weighing them, while you search for the
mark by which you may discover the drawn card.

53.—The Window Trick.

Place yourself in the recess of a window, and let
any one stand close to you, as near to the window as
possible. You now draw a card, hand it to him, and
request him to note it. This you must contrive to do

in such a manner, that you can catch a glimpse of the image of the card reflected in the window. You, now know what the card is as well as he does, and can point it out to him after the cards have been thoroughly shuffled.

54.—THE CARD OF ONE COLOUR FOUND IN A PACK OF THE OTHER.

Separate the pack into two parts, placing all the red cards in one pile, and all the black cards in the other. One of these packs you conceal in your pocket. You let any person draw a card from the other pack, and while he is examining the card, substitute the pack in your pocket for the one you hold in your hand. Let him place his card in the pack you have taken from your pocket, and shuffle as much as he pleases. On receiving back the pack, you will at once recognize the card he has drawn by the difference of colour.

55.—TO NAME SEVERAL CARDS WHICH HAVE BEEN DRAWN OUT OF A PACK WHICH HAS BEEN DIVIDED INTO TWO HEAPS.

For this trick you take a complete pack which has been divided into two such heaps that.all the aces, nines, sevens, fives, and threes are in one heap, and all the kings, queens, knaves, tens, eights, sixes, fours, and twos are in the other heap.

You now let several of the company draw cards out of either of the heaps, change the heaps unperceived, and let the person place the odd cards, as ace, nine, &c., into the heap of even cards, and VICE VERSA. On

running over the cards, you easily discover the drawn
cards, the even cards being in the heap of odd cards,
and the odd cards in the heap of even cards.

56—To find a Certain Card after it has been Shuffled in the Pack.

As you shuffle the cards, note the bottom one,
being careful not to shuffle it from its place. Then
let any one draw a card from the middle of the pack,
look at it, and place it on the top. Let him then cut
the pack. The card in question will be found in front
of the one which was at first the bottom card.

57.—Of Twenty-five Cards laid in Five Rows upon a Table to Name the One Touched.

To perform this trick you need a confederate. The
latter sits near the table, has both his hands closed,
and points out the card touched by the finger which
he leaves extended. The fingers of the right hand
indicate the cross rows counted from above downwards; the fingers of the left hand, on the contrary,
point out the number of the card in the cross row,
counting from left to right.

If, for example, the third card from the left in the
second cross row is the one touched, your accomplice
leaves the second finger of the right hand, and the
third finger of the left hand unbent, closing all the
others.

This must be done naturally, and not in too open a
manner, as it might easily be detected.

58.—Of Two Rows of Cards to tell the One Which has been Touched.

You lay two rows of cards upon the table, six or eight in each row. You have arranged with an accomplice that the upper cards, counted from the left signify days, the lower cards hours.

You now leave the room, requesting one of the company to touch a card. On returning you step to the table and begin to look for the card, when, after a while, your accomplice cries out, as if in mockery, "Yes, you might look for it three days, and never find it," if the touched card is the third card from the left in the upper row. You pay no attention, however, to his remark, but continue to search. At last you apparently lose your temper, and mix the cards together, exclaiming, "The cards are false to-day!" Then you reflect again, shuffle the cards, place them in two rows, and after some hesitation, point out the touched card.

59.—To Guess the Card Thought of.

To perform this trick, the number of cards must be divisible by 3, and it is more convenient that the number should be odd. Desire a person to think of a card; place the cards on the table with their faces downwards, and, taking them up in order, arrange them in three heaps, with their faces upwards, and in such a manner that the first card of the pack shall be first in the first heap, the second the first in the second heap, and the third the first in the third, the fourth the second in the first, and so on. When the

heaps are completed, ask the person in which heap
the card he thought of is, and when he tells you,
place that heap in the middle; then turning up the
packet, form three heaps as before, and again inquire
in which heap the card thought of is; form the three
heaps afresh, place the heap containing the card
thought of again in the centre, and ask which of
them contains the card. When this is known, place
it as before, between the other two, and again form
three heaps, asking the same question. Then take
up the heaps for the last time, put that containing the
card thought of in the middle, and place the packet
on the table with the faces downwards, turn up the
cards till you count half the number of those contained in the packet; twelve, for example, if there
be twenty-four, in which case the twelfth card will
be the one the person thought of. If the number of
the cards be at the same time odd, and divisible by
three, such as fifteen, twenty-one, twenty-seven, &c.,
the trick will be much easier, for the card thought of
will always be that in the middle of the heap in
which it is found the third time, so that it may be
easily distinguished without counting the cards; in
reality, nothing is necessary but to remember, while
you are arranging the heap for the third time, the
card which is the middle one of each. Suppose, for
example, that the middle card of the first heap be
the Ace of Spades, that the second be the King of
Hearts, and that the third be the Knave of Hearts;
if you are told that the heap containing the required
card is the third, that card must be the Knave of
Hearts. You may therefore have the cards shuffled,
without troubling them any more; and then, looking

them over for form's sake, may name the Knave of Hearts when it occurs.

60.—THE CIRCLE OF FOURTEEN CARDS.

To turn down fourteen cards which lie in a circle upon the table, observing to turn down only those cards at which you count the number seven.

To do this you must bear in mind the card which you first turn down. Begin counting from any card from one to seven, and turn the seventh card down. Starting with this card, you again count from one to seven, and turn the seventh card down, &c., &c. When you come to the card which you first turned down, you skip it, passing on to the next, and so on until all the cards are turned. This is a very entertaining trick.

61.—THE SHIFTING CARD.

Put at the top of your pack any card you please, say the Queen of Clubs. Make the pass, by which you put it in the middle of the pack and make some one draw it; cut again, and get the same card into the middle; make the pass again, to get it to the top of the pack, and then present it and get it drawn by a second person, who ought not to be so near the first as to be able to perceive that he has drawn the same. Repeat this process untill you have made five people draw the same card. Shuffle, without loosing sight of the Queen of Clubs, and, spreading on the table any four cards whatever with this queen, ask if every one sees his own card. They will reply in the

)

affirmative, since each sees the Queen of Clubs.
Turning over these cards, withdrawing the queen,
and approaching the first person, ask if that be his
card, taking care while showing it to him that the
others may not be able to see it. He will tell you it
is. Blow on it, or strike it, and show it to a second
person, and so on.

62.—THE MAGIC SLIDE, OR TO MAKE A CARD DIS-APPEAR IN AN INSTANT.

Divide the pack, placing one half in the palm of the
left hand, with the face of the cards downwards ; then
take the balance of the pack, in the right hand, holding them between the thumb and three first fingers,
and place the cards upright, so that the edges of the
cards in your right hand will rest upon the back of
those lying in the palm of the left hand perpendicularly and forming a right angle, by which you will
perceive that the four fingers of the left hand touch
the last card of the upright cards in your right
hand. Be sure you get this position correctly, for the
rest of the trick is very simple. You now request
any one of your audience to examine the top card of
the half pack that rests in the palm of your left hand,
and to replace it again. Having done this, you request him to look at it again, and to his amazement it
will have disappeared, and another card will appear
in its place.

To perform this trick, after you have assumed the
position already described, you must damp the tips of
the four fingers that rests against the last card of the
upright cards in your right hand. You must now

raise the upright cards in your right hand very quickly, and the last card will adhere to the damped fingers of your left hand.

As you raise the upright cards you must close your left hand skilfully, and you will thereby place the last card of the upright cards—which adheres to the fingers of your left hand—upon the top of the cards in the palm of your left hand, and when you request the person who examined the top card in your hand to look at it once more, he will see the card you have just placed there, instead of the one he first examined.

This is a capital sleight-of-hand trick, and with very little practice can be performed with great dexterity. The principal thing you must observe is to be very rapid and dexterous in slipping the card at the back of the upright card from its position there to the top of the cards in the palm of your left hand.

63.—The Four Transformed Kings.

You have the four kings of a pack, and have placed them in your hand in such a manner that one slightly overtops the other, yet so that each can easily be distinguished when held closely in the hand.

After showing them to the company, you slide them together, and place them, thus joined, upon the top of the pack, which you hold in your right hand. You then draw off the four top cards, and lay each in a person's lap, face downwards, directing them to place the flat of the hand upon them. You now draw four other cards from the pack, and place them each upon the lap of a neighbour of each of the four above persons, and direct them also to cover them with the flat of the hand. You now step with the rest of the cards in front of each of these eight persons, flirt the cards towards the lap of each, and when each lifts his card from his lap, and looks at it, it appears that the four persons upon whose lap you have placed the four kings have altogether different cards, and their neighbours have now the four kings.

This is done in the following manner:—While you are drawing the four kings from the pack, and placing them as described, one upon the other in your hand, you at the same time, unperceived, carry off four other cards, and place them behind the four kings, so that they lie in the hollow of your hand, and cannot be seen. When, after having shown the four kings, you push them together in a heap, the four kings, of course, come in front of the four other cards, which latter now lie on the top of the pack. These you distribute to the first four persons, and then deal out the four kings to their neighbors.

64.—TO GUESS THE SPOTS ON CARDS AT THE BOTTOM OF THREE PACKETS, WHICH HAVE BEEN MADE BY THE DRAWER.

Tell a person to choose, as he pleases, three cards from a Eucre pack, informing him that the ace counts for eleven, the picture cards for ten, and the others according to the number of spots. When he has chosen these three, tell him to put them on the table, and to place on each as many cards as spots are required to make fifteen. That is to say, in the example, eight cards would have to be put on the seven of clubs, four cards on the ace, and five above the ten. Let him return you the rest of the pack, and (while pretending to count something in them) count how many remain. Add sixteen to this number, and you will have the number of spots in the three bottom cards, as may be seen in this example, where

Seven of Clubs.   Ace of Diamonds.   Ten of Spades.

twelve cards remain, to which number add sixteen, and the amount (twenty-eight) is the number on the three cards.

65.—To Guess the Cards which Four Persons have fixed their Thoughts upon.

You take four cards, show them to the first person, request him to select one of them in thought, and lay them aside. Then take four other cards, let a second person choose one of them, place these four cards upon the table beside the first four, but a little apart. Proceed in the same way with the third and fourth person.

You now take the first person's four cards, and lay them separately, side by side. Upon these four cards you place the four cards of the second person in the same order, and so with the four cards of the third and fourth person.

You now show each pile to the four persons, one after the other, asking each in which pile he finds the card he has thought of.

As soon as you know this you discover the cards thought of in the following order: The card thought of by the first person is, of course, the first in the pile in which he says it is contained; the second person's card is the second of the pile, so also the third and fourth person's card is the third and fourth of the pile.

66 —*How to Arrange the Twelve Picture Cards and the Four Aces of a Pack in Four Rows, so that there will be in neither Row Two Cards of the same Value nor Two of the same Suit, whether counted horizontally or perpendicularly.*

The simplest way of performing this trick is to form a diagonal line from the left to the right with the four aces, as annexed figure. Then form another

[ ] Ace of Hearts.

[ ] Ace of Diamonds.

[ ] Ace of Spades.

[ ] Ace of Clubs.

diagonal line, from the right to the left, with the four knaves, crossing the preceding diagonal line, and you will have a position similar to this. This done, place a king and a queen in each of the four spaces which remain to be filled, in order to complete the

Knave of
Spades.

Knave of Clubs.

Knave of Hearts.

Knave of
Diamonds.

the square of four rows, being careful to choose the
suits, and to arrange the cards in such a manner as
to fulfil the conditions required. The cards will then
be arranged in the following order. By pursuing any

Q. of Clbs. K. of Dds.

Queen
of
Spades.

King of
Hearts.

King of
Clubs

Queen
of Dds.

K. of Spds. Q. of Hrts.

other method than the one above indicated, it will be found very difficult to fulfil the required conditions, and, at all events, it will take you a long time to do so.

67.—On Entering a Room, to Know of Three Cards placed Side by Side which have been reversed—that is to say, turned Upside Down.

This trick is a very easy one, as the two ends of the cards are cut so as to leave a margin of an unequal width. All that is requisite is to place all the broad ends of the cards either towards or from you, when, upon entering the room, you will at once perceive which card has been turned.

68.—To Bring a Card which has been Thrown Out of the Window into the Pack again.

After you have shuffled the pack and placed it upon the table, you let any person draw forth the lowest card, of which there are two alike, at the bottom of the pack; tear it in small pieces, and throw them out of the window.

You then assure the company that the pieces just thrown out will join themselves together again, and return as a whole card to the pack. You raise the window, call " Come, come, come!" Then approach the table, assuring the spectators that the mutilated card has returned complete to its old place in the pack; and let them satisfy themselves that such is the fact.

EXPERIMENTS BY CHEMISTRY,

FIREWORKS, &c.

———

* As there is some danger in performing tricks of this kind, they should be managed with extreme caution, and on no account be attempted by very young and inexperienced persons.

———

1.—To Obtain Fire from Water.

Throw a small quantity of potassium on the surface of a little water in a Basin. Immediately a rose-coloured flame will be produced. Any chemist will supply the quantity for several of these experiments for a very small sum.

2.—To Give a Party a Ghastly Appearance.

Take half a pint of spirits, and, having warmed it, put a handful of salt with it into a basin; then set it on fire, and it will have the effect of making every person look hideous. This feat must be performed in a room.

3.—The Fire and Wine Bottle.

Procure a tin bottle with a tube nearly as large as its neck, passing from the bottom of the neck to the bottom of the bottle, in which there must be a hole

of a size to correspond with it. Between the tube
and the neck of the bottle let there be sufficient space
to allow you to pour in some wine, which will remain
in the bottle outside the tube. Begin the trick by
pouring a glass of wine out of the bottle, through
which a confederate will thrust a burning fuzee into
the tube, so that, at your command, fire is emitted
from the mouth of the bottle. As soon as the fire is
extinguished, or withdrawn, you can take up the
bottle again, and pour out more wine.

4.—THE FIERY FLASH.

Let a quantity of minute iron filings drop upon the
flame of a candle from a sheet of paper about eight or
ten inches above it; as they descend in the flame, they
will enter into a vivid and sparkling combustion.

5.—TO BOIL A LIQUID WITHOUT FIRE.

Put into a thin phial two parts of oil of vitriol and
one part of water; by stirring them well together, the
mixture instantly becomes hot, and acquires a temper-
ature above that of boiling water.

6.—TO PROCURE HYDROGEN GAS.

Procure a phial with a cork stopper, through which
is thrust a piece of tobacco-pipe. Into the phial put
a few pieces of zinc, or small iron nails; on this pour
a mixture of equal parts of sulphuric acid (oil of vitriol) and water, previously mixed in a tea cup to pre-
vent accidents. Replace the cork stopper with the

piece of tobacco-pipe in it; the hydrogen gas will then be liberated thorugh the pipe in a small stream. Apply the flame of a candle or taper to this stream, and it will immediately take fire, and burn with a clear flame until all the hydrogen in the phial be exhausted. In this experiment the zinc or iron, by the action of the acid, becomes oxygenized, and is dissolved, thus taking the oxygen from the sulphuric acid and water; the hydrogen (the other constituent part of the water) is thereby liberated and ascends.

7.—To Copy Writing with a Flat-iron.

Mix a little sugar in the ink which is used for the writing. Lay a sheet of unsized paper, that is, soft white paper, damped with a sponge, on the written paper, and passing lightly over it a flat-iron, moderately heated, a copy may easily be taken.

8.—To make Fringe appear about the Flame of a Candle.

Procure two pieces of plate-glass, moisten two of their sides with water, put them together, and look through them at the candle, when you will perceive the flame surrounded with beautifully colored fringes. This is the effect of moisture intermixed with portions of air, and presents an appearance similar to dew.

9—To Produce Instantaneous Light upon Ice.

Throw upon ice a small piece of potassium, and it will burst into a bright flame.

10.--To MAKE PAPER FIREPROOF.

To accomplish this, dip a sheet of paper in a strong solution of alum water, and when dry repeat the process two or three times. When it is thoroughly dried, you may put it in the flame of a candle and it will not burn.

11.—To MELT LEAD IN PAPER.

Procure a very smooth ball of lead and wrap it up in a piece of paper, taking care that there be no wrinkles in it, and that it be everywhere in contact with the ball. Hold it in this state over the flame of a taper, and the lead will be melted without the paper being burnt. The lead, when once fused, will in a short time pierce the paper, and, of course, run through.

12.—To MELT STEEL AS EASILY AS LEAD.

With a pair of tongs or pincers hold a piece of steel in the fire till it is red hot, then touch it with a stick of brimstone, when the contact will cause the steel to melt and drop like a liquid.

13.—A LIGHT THAT BURNS FOR A YEAR.

Put a stick of phosphorus into a large dry phial, not corked, and it will give a light sufficient to discern any object in a room when placed close to it. If the phial be kept in a cool place, where there is no great current of air, its luminous appearance will be retained for several months.

14.—FLAME EXTINGUISHED BY GAS.

Place a lighted candle in a jar, and let carbonic gas be poured upon it from another jar. In a few seconds the flame will be extinguished, though the eye is incapable of observing that anything is poured out.

15.—THE TOBACCO-PIPE CANNON.

Take of saltpetre one ounce, cream of tartar one ounce, sulphur half an ounce, beat them to powder separately, then mix them together. Put a grain into a pipe of tobacco, and when it is lighted it will give the report of a musket, without breaking the pipe. By putting as much as may lie on your nail in a piece of paper, and setting fire to it, tremendous reports will be the result.

16.—PRINCE RUPERT'S DETONATING GLASS BOMBS.

These may be made in the following manner:—Drop some small pieces of common green glass, while red hot, into cold water, when they will assume a tear-like form. The spherical portion will bear very rough treatment, but the instant the smallest particle of the tail be broken off the whole flies into countless fragments. Many experiments may be performed with these curious drops, but, being attended with danger, are omitted here.

17.—TO WASH THE HANDS IN MOLTEN LEAD.

Take one ounce of quicksilver, two ounces of good

boleammoniac, half an ounce of camphor, and two
ounces of aqua-vitae; mix them together, and put
them into a brazen mortar, beating them with a pestle.
Rub the hands all over with this ointment, and they
may be put into melted lead with impunity: the metal
being poured upon them will neither burn nor scald.

18.—To make an Artificial Earthquake and Volcano.

Mix equal parts of pounded sulphur and iron filings, and having formed the whole into a paste with
water, bury a certain quantity of it (forty or fifty
pounds, for example) at about the depth of a foot below the surface of the earth.   In ten or twelve hours
after, if the weather be warm, the earth will swell
and burst, and throw up flame, which will enlarge
the aperture, scattering around a yellow and blackish
dust.

19.—To Produce Fire from Cane.

The Chinese rattans, which are used when split for
making cane chairs, will, when dry, if struck against
each other, give fire; and are used accordingly in
some places in lieu of flint and steel.

20.—To Soften Iron or Steel.

Either of the following simple methods will make
iron or steel as soft as lead:—
  1. Take a little clay, cover your iron with it, temper it in a charcoal fire.

2. When the iron or steel is red hot, strew helle-bore on it.

3. Quench the iron or steel in the juice or water of common beans.

21.—To Fill with Smoke Two Apparently Empty Bottles.

Rinse out one bottle with hartshorn, and another bottle with spirit of salt; next bring the bottles to-gether mouth to mouth; both will at once be pervad-ed with white vapours. The vapours in question are composed of sal ammoniac—a solid body generated by the union of two invisible gases.

22.—To Make Luminous Writing in the Dark.

Fix a small piece of solid phosphorus in a quill, and write with it upon paper; if the paper be then placed in a dark room the writing will appear beautifully lu-minous.

23.—To Make Red Fire.

The beautiful red fire which is used in the theatres is composed of the following ingredients: Forty parts of dry nitrate of strontian, thirteen parts of finely powdered sulphur, five parts of chlorate of potash, and four parts of sulphuret of antimony.

24.—To Make Green Fire.

Take of flour of sulphur thirteen parts, of nitrate of

baryta seventy-seven, of oxymuriate of potassia five, of metallic arsenic two, of charcoal three. The nitrate of baryta should be well dried and powdered.

25.—To Make Wine or Brandy Float on Water.

To perform this seeming impossibility, take a tumbler half-full of water, and placing a piece of thin muslin over the top of the same, gently strain the brandy or wine through the muslin, and it will remain on the top of the water.

26.—To Make Beautiful Transparent Coloured Water.

The following liquors, which are coloured, being mixed, produce colours very different from their own. The yellow tincture of saffron and the red tincture of roses, when mixed, produce a green. Blue tincture of violets and brown spirit of sulphur produce a crimson. Red tincture of roses and brown spirits of hartshorn make a blue. Blue tincture of violets and blue solution of copper give a violet colour. Blue tincture of cyanus and blue spirit of sal ammoniac, coloured, make green. Blue solution of Hungarian vitriol and brown lye of potash make yellow. Blue solution of Hungarian vitriol and red tincture of roses make black. Blue tincture of cyanus and green solution of copper, produce red.

in which he says it is contained; the second person's card is the second of the pile, so also the third and fourth person's card is the third and fourth of the pile.

TRICKS WITH COINS.

How to Make a Coin Stick against the Wall.

Take a small coin, such as a shilling or a halfpenny, and on the edge cut a small notch with a knife, so that a little point of the metal will project. By pressing this against a door or wooden partition, the coin will remain mysteriously adhering against the perpendicular surface.

The Balancing Coin.

To perform this experiment procure a bottle, cork it, and in the cork place a needle in a perpendicular position. Now take another cork, and cut a slit in it, so that the edge of a shilling will fit into the nick ; next stick two forks into the cork with the handles in a sloping position downwards, and placing the edge of the coin on the needle, it will spin round about without falling off. The reason is this,—the weight of the forks, projecting as they do much below the coin, brings the centre of gravity much below the point of suspension, or the point of the needle, and therefore the coin remains perfectly safe and upright.

The Vanishing Coin.

This is a clever trick, and may be done with good effect in the following manner :—Previously stick a small piece of white wax on the nail of your middle finger, lay a sixpence on the palm of your hand, and state to the company that you will make it vanish at the word of command, at the same time observing that many persons perform the feat by letting the sixpence fall into their sleeve, but to convince them that you have not recourse to any such deception, turn up your cuffs. Then close your hand, and by bringing the waxed nail in contact with the sixpence, it will firmly adhere to it. Then blow upon your hand and cry " Begone ;" and suddenly opening it, and extending your palm, you show that the sixpence has vanished. Care must be taken to remove the wax from the sixpence before restoring it to the owner, if it should have been borrowed from one of the company.

TO BRING TWO SEPARATE COINS INTO ONE HAND.

Take two halfpence, which must be carefully placed in each hand ; the right hand with the coin on the third and little finger, and the left hand with the coin on the palm. Then place at a short distance from each other both hands open on the table, the left palm being level with the fingers of the right. By now suddenly turning the hands over, the halfpenny from the right hand will fly, without being perceived, into the palm of the left, and make the transit appear most unaccountable to the bewildered eyes of the spectator. By placing the audience in front, and not at the side of the exhibitor, this illusion, if neatly performed, can never be detected.

THE MAGIC COIN.

Although a purely sleight-of-hand trick, it requires but little practice to perform it with dexterity. Take a shilling between the thumb and forefinger of the right hand ; then, by a rapid twist of the fingers, twirl the coin by the same motion that you would use to spin a teetotum, at the same time rapidly close your hand, and the coin will disappear up your coat-sleeve ; you can now open your hand, and, much to the astonishment of your audience, the coin will not be there. This capital trick may be varied in a hundred ways. One good way is to take three shillings, and, concealing one in the palm of your left hand, place the other two, one each between the thumb and forefinger of each hand, then give the coin in the right hand the twirl as already described, and, closing both hands quickly, the coin in the right hand will disappear up your sleeve, and the left hand, on being unclosed, will be found to contain two shillings, whilst that which *was* in the right will have disappeared. Thus you will make the surprised spectators believe that you conjured the coin from the right hand into the left.

THE HAT AND SHILLING TRICK.

Place a hat over a tumbler, the side of the hat resting on the top of the tumbler, and a shilling on the upper side of the hat; then, after making several feints, as if you intended to strike the hat upon the *rim*, give the hat a sharp quick blow upon the *inside*, and the coin will fall into the tumbler. This is a beautiful trick, if skilfully performed.

TO TAKE A SHILLING OUT OF A HANDKERCHIEF.

Conceal in your palm, or where your hand can easily get it, a common curtain ring. Spread on the table a handkerchief, and wrap up a shilling in it. Open out the handkerchief to convince the spectators that there is no deception, slip in the curtain ring, removing the shilling; and while the person is eagerly holding the handkerchief, with his eyes on the circular form of the shilling, take the opportunity of putting it aside into a hat or elsewhere. When you take up the handkerchief again, contrive to slip away the ring.

To Change a Sixpence into a Half-Sovereign.

Take two square pieces of paper, such as druggists use for making up powders, fold them up in a similar manner, pasting the backs together, and in one side place a half-sovereign. Show the spectators the side which is empty; borrow a sixpence, place it in the paper and fold it up; then say,—" With the touch of my magic wand, which has the virtue of the " Philosopher's stone." I change the sixpence into a half-sovereign." Tapping the paper, and turning it round with a flourish in the air, you open it at the side which contains the half-sovereign. To show your power of reconverting gold into silver, fold the paper up again, give it a tap with the other end of the wand, and after a similar flourish in the air, open it and deliver the sixpence to the owner.

The Magic Halfpenny.

Procure a small round box, about one inch deep, and of the same diameter as a halfpenny, line it with crimson, pasting a piece of the same paper on one side of a halfpenny, so that, when lying in the box, it will appear as if there was nothing there. Borrow a halfpenny from one of the company, substitute the prepared one for it, and, placing it in the box, shut the lid, and shake it up and down to let the spectators know by the sound that the coin is there. Now command it to disappear, and shake the box sideways; as the coin is made to fit the box accurately no noise is heard; the coin seems to be gone—to prove which open the box, and dislay the interior; the paper on the coin conceals it, and you can then direct the audience to look in any ornament or other place in the room, where you have previously hidden another halfpenny, which they will mistake for the one borrwed.

To Multiply Coin.

Inform the company that you can, by the exercise of your magical powers, increase sixpence to eighteen-pence before their eyes. To effect this, borrow a six-pence, get a tumbler of water and a plate; put the six-pence into the glass, and then, covering it with the plate, invert it on the table; the coin will appear on the plate to be a shilling, while the sixpence will seem the be floating on the top at the same time.

The Sixpence and Half-Crown in a Glass.

Place a sixpence in the bottom of a conical shaped glass, and over the latter place a half-crown. The puzzle is to remove the small coin from beneath the larger one, without touching either of the coins, or touching or upsetting the glass.

Blow with considerable force down one side of the glass upon the edge of the half crown. The sixpence will be expelled by the force of the air, and will fall either upon the upper surface of the half-crown, or upon the table. A little practice will render the performance of this feat very easy.

The Dinner Table Puzzle.

Lay a sixpence between two half-crowns, and place upon the larger coins a tumbler. Remove the sixpence without displacing either of the half-crowns, or the glass.

After having placed the tumbler and coins as indi-cated, simply scratch the table-cloth with the nail of the fore-finger, in the direction you would have the six-pence to move, and it will answer immediately. The table-cloth is necessary—for this reason the trick is best suited to the breakfast or dinner-table.

To Make a Sixpence Vanish.

The performer, who on all occasions should endeavor to keep his audience ignorant of what he is going to show, begins by inquiring which of the company can hold a sixpence securely in his hand. He selects one, and bidding him extend the palm of his right hand, places the coin in its centre, pressing it so hard with the thumb, that the impression will be retained a few seconds. Regaining the sixpence with his finger and thumb, he must jerk his arm up and down twic or thrice, and at the last movement of the hand above his head, the exhibitor should adroitly conceal the six-pence in his hair when bringing the hand down again ; and, pretending to place the coin in the palm, which must be instantly closed, the sixpence will have seem-ed to have vanished. The delusion may be completed by the operator putting his hat on his head, and after allowing time for conjecture, command the coin to appear in the hat, where, by slightly inclining the head, and removing the hat, it will of course be found and identified by the company.

THE END.

SOLON SHINGLE'S

JOKE BOOK

NEW YORK:

FREDERIC A. BRADY, PUBLISHER

26 ANN STREET.

www.ingramcontent.com/pod-product-compliance
Lightning Source LLC
Chambersburg PA
CBHW021224260626
47172CB00002B/587